SUBMARINE KILLER

Titles in this series

AAL CHRISTIANSEN

SUBMARINE KILLER

Collins
LONDON AND GLASGOW

First published 1967

PRINTED AND MADE IN GREAT BRITAIN BY
WM. COLLINS SONS AND CO. LTD.
LONDON AND GLASGOW

CONTENTS

1. No time to fight

NOTHING could have been less warlike than the Mediterranean that morning. The April sun was shining from a cloudless sky, and the water was the blue which most people only see on holiday posters. The *Alice*, in peace-time a 550 ton fishing trawler, was leaving a wake behind her as straight as a printer's rule. She had made that straight line ever since she left Malta, and her speed had not faltered. Whatever the morning looked like, the *Alice* had a date which she had to keep.

On the after-deck the depth-charge crews were finishing their cleaning of mechanism which was already clean. The Oerlikon gunners and the men who manned the twin-barrelled 0.5 in. machine guns were finished and awaiting the "stand down" so that they could light their first cigarettes of the morning. The crew of the twelve-pounder gun in the bows had already finished.

In the cubby-hole beneath the wheel-house the Asdic operator was sitting like a man in a dream. He was supposed to have the " cushiest " job aboard, with nothing to do but sit and wait for a submarine to come near.

Slugger Burton hated his job on the Asdic. Before the war he had been sitting for his mate's ticket, with the idea that one day he would command a ship like the *Alice* and go after fish off Bear Island, or maybe in the colder waters west of Spitzbergen.

He did not look like a slugger, but the nickname had come his way within two weeks of joining the Navy. There had been a boxing tournament, and for the fun of it, Geoffrey Burton had put his name down. Before he walked round to collect his trophy as lightweight champion of the shore estab-lishment, he was Slugger to everyone. It took him sixteen and a half minutes to get through to the final and dispose of five opponents. He won his championship bout in a few seconds under three minutes.

Slugger was cocking an eye at the clock and thinking of a cup of coffee when the monotonous pinging in his earphones suddenly changed. He began to get a solid echo.

The dreamy expression of a few seconds before vanished. His hand went out to adjust his set. The Asdic sent out electric impulses and if they encountered anything in their path, they bounced back to make those warning metallic sounds in his headset. Slugger knew he was on to a submarine!

A few moments later he had a forefinger on a button which warned the wheel-house that he wanted to speak to them.

"Got a contact, sir; about a thousand yards' range, bearing red sixty."

"Keep on it," was the curt retort.

A few moments later the *Alice* came to swift life as the alarm bells rang out and men raced to action stations. The crew of the twelve-pounder gun in the bows had their anti-flash gear on and their steel helmets in place seconds before the Oerlikon gunners had scrambled into their seats. The twelve-pounder crew were always johnny-on-the-spot when *action stations* sounded.

In the engine-room the stand-by had been

given, and young David Cochran, the sub-lieutenant second-in-command of the *Alice*, had made a note in the log and marked a spot on the chart before Lieutenant Otis Chambers, skipper of the *Alice* had come up from his cabin to the wheel-house.

"Contact at a thousand yards, sir, bearing red sixty," he said. "I haven't changed course at all. I didn't know whether you'd want to attack."

"I don't," Chambers said curtly. He was a tall, grizzled man, who had served in mine-sweepers in the First World War, and had been an amateur yachtsman ever since. Otis had never had to worry about earning his bread and butter, and years of yachting had made him a poor conversationalist. He spoke when he had to.

A few moments later Slugger Burton in the Asdic room was calling the bridge again.

"Contact swinging to port, sir. Range now six hundred yards. Seems to be closing in fast."

Otis Chambers and David Cochran exchange quick glances.

"Italian for a pound," Chambers said

icily. "Anybody with any guts would surface and knock us for six with his guns. This fellow is going to get into position for a torpedo. Blast him. We'll have to attack —and that's the last thing I wanted to do."

He gave an order to the man at the wheel, then flipping the switch of the loud hailer gave the order:

"Set D for Dog." That was for the men handling the depth-charges. It meant they were to fire ten depth-charges and the big canisters of deadly Amatol would be fused to explode at three distinct depths. The first ones would blast the depths at 600 feet, the next four at 400 feet, and the last two at 250 feet. Any submarine in the area and between those depths would get at the least a very rough shaking.

"Out pins," Chambers ordered, and his voice was as calm and steady as if he were ordering a glass of sherry. A few moments later the Petty Officer responsible for depth-charging bawled back:

"Pins out!"

In the few moments while this had been taking place the *Alice*, trembling a little more as she clocked up an extra knot, was now bows on to the contact. In his cubby-hole Slugger Burton was keyed up, whispering into his mouthpiece the news which his intricate mechanism was bringing him. The contact was now just 400 yards away, and she, too, would have a "listener" who would be able to hear the thud-thud-thud of the *Alice*'s single screw. He would be warning his commander that the surface ship was tearing in to the attack.

"Red fifty now, sir. Red fifty at three hundred yards . . . and moving to red forty."

In the wheel-house Otis Chambers gave a quick order to the helmsman and the *Alice* heeled a little under a quick spin of the wheel. A breathless fifty seconds passed before Slugger announced:

"Contact, sir." That was the moment. It meant that they were actually passing over the submarine. Otis Chambers stared straight ahead, and David Cochran knew that this grizzle-haired man was counting to himself. He was trying to ensure that when he gave the order "Fire!" they would drop their depth charges directly over the spot where the submarine was. A bull's-eye meant a dead sub.

"Fire!" The loud-hailer fairly crackled with the command, and almost at once the first depth charges slid over the stern and plopped into the sea. The first spout of foam had not fallen back before the next lot went in. Now they could only wait, and hope.

"All gone, sir," David Cochran announced, for he had been on the bridge-wing staring back towards the stern. At once the wheel was put hard over again. They would come round in a semi-circle and drop another stick of depth-charges.

All on board the trim little vessel were tense; none more so than the men in the engine-room. They would get a kick from the underwater explosions, and many a chief engineer had found himself with hours of repair work after a depth-charge attack. A thump on the ship's bottom could so shake the equipment that something broke . . . often enough in the ship's electrical gear.

The last two depth-charges exploded first, for they were set for 250 feet. The sea suddenly erupted. Then came the dull thud of a double explosion, followed by two greater explosions as the charges set at 400 and 600 feet exploded.

The *Alice* charged slightly to one side of the disturbed water, and a second pattern of depth-charges went down to churn up the sea until it looked like new milk.

" Still got him, sir," Slugger called up to the bridge, " but very faint. He's not moving at all."

For a few moments Otis Chambers stood chewing at his lower lip, then he shrugged and ordered the helmsman to put the *Alice* back on her original course.

" That's given him a scare," he said grimly. " We can't waste time on him."

" Shall I stand the men down, sir?" Cochran asked.

" Yes . . . er . . . no, wait a minute. Call them for'ard. They'll be wondering why we're not finishing off this scrap. I'll speak to them."

A few minutes later the gun crews were assembled in the sunshine on the port side of the wheel-house. Otis Chambers came on to the bridge-wing and stood for a moment looking down on them. His powerful binoculars were still slung round his neck, and his voice was a little less curt than usual when he said:

"It isn't often I explain my actions, men. No doubt you are wondering why we didn't follow the usual practice of standing by to finish off this sub. There's a good reason; we have more urgent business to attend to. The Army is pulling out of Greece." He stood looking down at his deck crew for a moment, the merest suggestion of a smile crinkling the corners of his mouth. Then he added: "We have the task of picking up wounded men from a beach in the South Peloponnesus."

Alfie Price, who had sailed in more fishing trawlers than anyone, and been booted off them all for incompetence, whispered:

"South Pel . . . wot?"

For a moment the little quiver at the corners of Otis Chambers's mouth curved into a real smile as he said:

"If you had studied your Greek history a little more, Price, you would know that the Peloponnesus is the southern tip of Greece

—like a large island. You probably remember now?"

"Yessir," Alfie lied. "Yessir, it's come back to me now."

"I thought it would," Otis chuckled, then his expression hardened again. "We have let that sub off the hook because we are already late. The evacuation has been going on for some time. All ships have to be away from the beaches by three in the morning. The German bombers have already inflicted damage. Ships not away from the coast in good time—that is by three in the morning —are likely to be heavily bombed. We are in a hurry . . . so we do not have time to waste on an Italian submarine. We may have a chance to finish her off some other time. That is all."

The crew stood down. Guns were unloaded, and the depth-charge crew cleaned their slides and rails, and brought up more charges to fill the racks again. The *Alice* plugged eastwards; but now she was quivering just that little bit more than usual.

She was now touching eleven and a half

knots and her chief engineer was cocking an anxious eye at his steam gauges. Otis Chambers wanted to make up the half hour he had lost in depth-charging the unseen submarine; but when a ship has been at full stretch, making up a lost half hour is not easy.

For ninety minutes the ship steamed eastwards. The crew had had their cigarettes and Slugger Burton had come off watch when the second alarm came. The man who had taken Slugger's place in the Asdic cubbyhole had another contact. It was only a faint contact from something well astern of them, but in the next half hour it grew gradually stronger. Despite the eleven and a half knots the *Alice* was doing, the submarine was gradually overhauling her.

"Well, David, what would you do if you were in my shoes?" Otis Chambers asked suddenly. The latest Asdic report showed that their pursuer was edging to starboard and was less than a thousand yards away. "No, think! We're walking a razor's edge. If we can keep up this speed, we'll get to G beach just after sunset, which is the time we are expected. If we stop and fight this Italian we could be an hour late."

"Is an hour vital, sir?" David asked.

"We've at least a hundred men to take off the beach," Chambers told him. "There could be more—numbers have a habit of growing when an army is being evacuated. I understand that many of them are either wounded or exhausted by hard fighting and forced marches. It could take us several hours to get them off—and the deadline at G beach is three in the morning. If you leave it later than that, German bombers could sink you. Now . . . what would you do?" and there was a hint of a twinkle in his usually serious grey-blue eyes.

"Well, sir, if we just keep running, the sub. is going to get in position on our flank, then send a couple of tin fish at us." He shrugged before adding: "If I were in your shoes—and I must admit I'm glad I'm not at this moment—I'd stand and fight."

Otis Chambers stroked his thin, aristocratic nose for a moment, then said:

" I never thought the day would come when I'd run away from a fight—but it has. Even if he attacks us, David, we keep on course. I want every man at action stations, and so long as we know he is on the starboard side, every man will keep a watch for torpedoes. That's how he'll try and get us. He hasn't the guts to surface and sink us by gun-fire."

Slugger Burton returned to the Asdic cubby-hole. When there was an alert on, the Asdic watch changed every two hours, so that no man got too tired to concentrate.

Half an hour after Slugger took over, when the submarine had closed to 500 yards on the starboard side, and tension on the *Alice* was at peak, there was a sudden chorus of warning yells. Keen eyes had spotted the tell-tale streak of bubbles rising to the surface. At least one torpedo was coming at them.

If Otis Chambers had not been so desperately anxious to get to G beach he would have turned and headed for the submarine, but in the secret orders he had picked up at

Malta there had been firm instructions not to engage in any action with the enemy, whether surface or underwater craft. The men on G beach were more important than anything else.

The wheel spun merrily and the steam steering purred and hissed. The *Alice* had always been lively in answering the helm, and she heeled as she turned to port, away from the submarine.

The torpedo missed by a score of yards, running just ahead of the Britisher. Had she not turned, the tin fish would have got her amidships, and that would have been the end of the *Alice* and her crew. A torpedo hit on a 550 ton craft would just about blow her apart.

The yells of glee from the *Alice*'s crew as they saw the torpedo running on towards the Adriatic stopped abruptly when there came a single alarm call of:

" She's surfacing . . . submarine surfacing astern."

The Italian submarine commander was not quite the spineless idiot Otis Chambers had imagined. He had been running at

At least one torpedo was coming at them . . .

periscope depth for the past ten minutes, and when he fired his first torpedo, his gun crews were crowding in the conning tower.

The moment his periscope mirrors showed him that the *Alice* was turning away to avoid the torpedo, the signal was given to surface. With her diesels switched on at full speed and her hydroplanes tilted to give her maximum upward thrust, she surged forward and up, the sea boiling all around as compressed air spewed the water from her ballast tanks.

The moment the conning tower broke surface men scrambled out and rushed to the guns. There was a large calibre gun for'ard of the conning tower, twin 0.5 machine guns aft of the conning tower and a machine gun in the conning tower itself.

While the submarine was still sluicing tons of water off her whaleback, her gun crew loaded, sighted and fired their first round. Not often does a gunner register a bull with his first round, but either the Italian gun-layer was a wizard or it was his lucky day.

It seemed no more than a second after the flash and the puff of smoke from the submarine that the *Alice* trembled. There was a hard cracking report, then her wheel-house top sailed into the air and fell into the sea.

Short of a hit in the engine-room, where a ship's heart beats, the wheel-house is the next vital spot, for there the brains of the ship assemble—and the shell had gone home in that very spot.

2. Target practice for a sub

FOR THE CREW of the *Alice* the next minute or so was like a sudden trip to Hell itself. The Italian submarine had stopped now, and not only was the for'ard gun firing, but the men at the machine guns were pouring a withering hail of steel-jacketed bullets at the unlucky *Alice*. When these hit, they scattered fragments of hot metal in a deadly hail.

The plates of the *Alice* chattered and trembled under the barrage and twice in the next minutes there was the crump as a shell went home. When the first shell exploded as it struck the wheel-house top, the helmsman had just begun to spin the wheel back to bring the rudder amidships. This would have put the vessel on a straight course again. But the steam steering continued to turn wheel and rudder, for the helmsman was dead. The *Alice*, instead of continuing to head directly away from the Italian, now started to swing to starboard, presenting herself broadside to the submarine's guns.

In the Asdic cubby-hole Slugger Burton had been thrown off his seat when the shell exploded above. What was more, the little hatch which enabled him to go directly into the wheel-house was blown in by the force of the explosion. When he got to his feet he was choking and gasping in the fumes.

He tried to leave by the door, but it was jammed. Half-blinded and gasping for breath, he turned and scrambled up the six-runged ladder into what remained of the wheel-house.

A sheaf of papers pinned to the rear wall of the wheel-house was burning. The helmsman lay crumpled behind the wheel. Lieutenant Chambers was face down on the floor and young David Cochran was huddled in a corner.

Crump! Another shell from the Italian burst on the foredeck and shrapnel smashed into the front of the wheel-house, one piece coming through the gap where an armoured glass window had been. It crashed into the woodwork behind Slugger and within seconds the planking began to burn.

From the bows where the twelve-pounder crew were crouching came a bellowed plea:

"Turn us to face 'em, sir."

Someone had seen a movement in the wheel-house and thought either Chambers or Cochran had risen from the wreckage to take command again.

Slugger was dazed and still gasping for breath, but he started to turn the wheel. Two spokes had been smashed out of the wheel and a sliver of shining brass had been ripped off by a shell fragment, but it was still working.

"What are they all doing?" Slugger snarled, wondering why the *Alice* was not hitting back. Then *boomph!* The crew of the twelve-pounder, ignoring the devil's tattoo of 0.5 bullets spraying the air around them, fired their first round. The breech block was swung out and the smoking shell-case bounced off the gun platform on to the foredeck. A fresh round was slammed home at the same instant that a cloud of spray masked the Italian submarine's conning tower.

Lady Luck must have decided to lend a hand to friend and foe alike that day. The Italian's first shell had struck a deadly blow at the *Alice*; now the twelve-pounder gun from the *Alice* dropped its first shell at the base of the Italian's conning tower.

"That's it," Slugger screeched. "Give it to them, Georgie."

The *Alice* was still swinging on half rudder and he had to give her opposite rudder to bring her bow on to the submarine. Again the twelve-pounder thumped, but this time the shell whistled over the conning tower. It was a moment when the battle hung in the balance. Only the *Alice's* twelve-pounder was in action. If the machine gunners on the submarine had concentrated their fire on the bows of the Britisher, they could have wiped out the gun's crew in thirty seconds.

The *Alice* was now surging through the water, and Slugger had steadied her on a collision course. Though there was a gaping hole in her side and an equally big hole in her midship decking through which smoke and flames were billowing, the engines were still thrumming and there was a nice little curl of foam at her bows.

Another minute, or ninety seconds at the most, and there would be a crunch and scream of metal on metal as the *Alice* thrust herself on to the submarine's hull.

Slugger stood behind the wheel, staring ahead through the glassless window-frames, while behind him the woodwork of the wheel-house crackled and burned. He had no thought of altering course, and it was the submarine commander's nerve which finally broke.

From the depths of the sub the harsh wailing of a klaxon sounded, and as if they had been waiting for that signal, the gun crews left their weapons and fought one another to get to the conning-tower hatch. The long, sleek, whale-like submarine began to move forward and down. She was making a desperate crash dive to avoid a collision.

Water and air boiled as her vents were opened wide to fill her buoyancy tanks. The elevator fins were at maximum tilt, this time to take her below the surface, and she was sliding forward and down while five men still fought to get into the conning-tower.

Another round from the twelve-pounder flashed across her hull, missing it by what seemed no more than inches. She was sinking lower all the time, and as the *Alice* ploughed up and over the spot where a minute earlier the enemy had been, there was no more than a greenish shape in the water below and a swirl from her screws.

" Fire . . . fire!" Slugger screamed, grabbing at the loud-hailer microphone; but there was no booming command to ring over the battered *Alice.* That first shell which had silenced the men in the wheel-house had also put the loud-hailer out of action.

When no depth-charges rolled into the sea, Slugger bounded down to the deck and started to run aft. He went half a dozen paces, then stopped. For the first time he got an idea of the kind of punishment the ship had taken. At his feet were the crew of the Oerlikon gun.

Their weapon lay with its twisted muzzle across the low rail. Ahead of him was the hole in the deck, with oily smoke and flames belching upwards. In less than ten minutes, a trim little anti-submarine vessel had been churned and blasted into a shambles.

He turned back to the wheel-house when he heard shouts from the bows. The twelve-pounder gun's crew were coming running, eyes blazing with triumph. They knew they had driven the Italian off, but their gleeful expressions changed when they realised what a hammering the *Alice* had taken. The battle had been at almost point blank range, and the Italian gun crews had not wasted their opportunity.

Remembering the fire in the wheel-house, Slugger rushed back there. The wall extinguisher was on the floor, but it was in working order. He sluiced the planking, and the moment the fire was out, rushed down to the deck again. The rest of the canister he aimed into the billowing smoke and flames coming from below.

For the next hour, with the engines stopped, four men, Slugger, Big George, Porky Warren and Alfie Price of the twelve-pounder gun, fought the flames below, side by side with the chief and second engineer, and the two stokers. They wore breathing masks, and when the last flames died down the eight men were very near collapse.

They crawled up on deck and gaped at the change which had come over the scene. In the stern, stretched out in rows, were the dead and the injured. One or two had been bandaged and were sitting up sucking feebly at cigarettes.

Before they could begin to ask questions, Hodgy appeared. He was a veteran of the First World War—in fact the jokers sometimes insisted that he had been at the siege of Mafeking. A lean little man with silvery hair, he was the *Alice*'s cook. He came along the port side of the deck, somehow supporting Lieutenant Otis Chambers—an Otis Chambers who presented a dreadful sight. There was blood all over his face.

"Strike a light!" Slugger forgot his weariness, and hurrying forward helped Hodgy with his burden.

"Lay him down gently," Hodgy ordered. "I think he's got a bit of shell in his thigh, or something."

"I'm not dying." The words made Slugger start in surprise. Otis Chambers looked just about ready to die, but his voice was hardly altered. There was not even the suggestion of a shake in it. The words were crisp and there was almost the hint of a chuckle in them as Slugger continued to gape. The youngster had seen a fair amount of action, but this was the first time he had come face to face with a man who looked so terribly smashed-up.

"Most of it will wash off," Otis Chambers said as they laid him gently on deck. "It's a scalp wound, that's all. I always said we should have a different shape of steel helmet. Mind my leg, that's where the real damage is."

"What's he made of?" Big George asked in a whisper as they moved away to see if the two others in the wheel-house were still alive. "Y'know, Slugger, I never had much time for him. You expect the skipper to stand apart—but he always struck me as being a bit too stuck-up. Strike a light, though . . . he's got guts. Lumme!" and he shook his head.

For the next two hours the *Alice* lay rocking gently on the sunlit sea while the uninjured of her crew, nine in all, made an effort to clean up the ship. She had been mauled. Her bilges were full of fuel oil from a tank which had been ripped open by a shell, the same shell which started the fire. Of her armament, there was only the twelvepounder left intact. That and her depthcharges.

The Oerlikons and the machine guns were so much scrap metal. Had they taken a shell below the waterline nothing could have saved them. Of them all Hodge—or Hodgy as they called him—seemed the least shaken. He showed a new side then, for he doctored the injured and his calmness steadied the others.

When all had been done that could be done for the wounded, Hodgy made a kettle of tea. It was strong, and there was lots of milk and sugar in it. When Big George came forward with his hands dangling cups from every finger, Hodgy held up a hand and winked knowingly. Then, kneeling by the side of Otis Chambers he said:

"Beg pardon, sir, permission to splice the mainbrace?"

Otis Chambers had been lying with his eyes closed. There was an unusual pallor to his cheeks and shadows under his eyes. He was in pain and he had lost a lot of blood. Yet there was some iron in him yet, for when he opened his eyes and spoke, his voice did not lack firmness as he asked:

"Splice the mainbrace, Hodge? What for? In any case I have a taste in my mouth which suggests you have already been at the rum."

"Yessir, I gave you a tot, but that was for medicinal purposes, sir," Hodge said respectfully. "All the wounded have had rum, sir. I'm asking permission now for the uninjured. To celebrate, if you know what I mean, sir."

"I don't. What is there to celebrate?"

That took the wind out of even Hodge's sails for a moment. Then he murmured:

"We're alive, sir. We could have been dead!"

"You don't splice the mainbrace when you've been given a hammering," Otis

He opened his eyes—and spoke . . .

Chambers said firmly. "You'll tell Petty Officer Warren to issue rum—for medicinal purposes only. Half a cup per man, as and when required." For a moment Hodge gaped, for this icicle of an officer had winked at him.

The rum in the tea gave the uninjured the bracer they needed. After a short rest the wounded were carried below and made as comfortable as possible. Sub-Lieutenant David Cochran was still unconscious though there was no sign of a wound. A piece of shell had struck him on top of his steel helmet, and Hodge was of the opinion that their second-in-command was suffering from no more than severe concussion.

"Be right as a trivet in a few days," he said cheerfully.

"I've heard folks say that before," Bill Brown, the chief engineer, said, looking with disgust at an oil-soaked packet of cigarettes he had taken from the breast pocket of his overalls. "What I'm worrying about is how we get back to Malta, or across to Alex. We've about four hours' oil fuel . . . and no more."

The sun was setting when they were called to the skipper's cabin. Otis Chambers's head was swathed in bandages and there was a three inch board from his ankle to his armpit. Hodge had strapped the leg at intervals of six inches and for the first time ever the skipper of the *Alice* had taken orders from an able seaman. He was to lie completely still. His thigh was broken, and the only way to ensure that he would one day walk again was to obey orders.

By the time the black gang and the A.B.s had crowded into the cabin there was little room for anyone else. Lieutenant Otis Chambers lay in his bunk, and despite his heavily bandaged head, he still had the look of a master about him.

He wasted no time.

"When we left Malta we were under orders to proceed to a secret destination— G beach. If you look at that chart you'll see that the Peloponnesus is shaped like a hand, with three fingers and a thumb. Between them they make three big bays. Our destination, G beach, is in the first of these bays. It's not an ordinary bay. It's about thirty miles across the mouth and runs rather more than that distance in. I've marked G beach by a pencilled cross. We should be there now. I've already told you the Army is pulling out of Greece. We're under orders to pick up a hundred men from G beach." He paused for a moment and his lips tightened as if he were fighting back a grimace of pain. "There are some cigarettes on that shelf. Help yourselves."

When they were all smoking Otis Chambers said :

"The chief engineer tells me we have fuel for about four hours' steaming. We can get to G beach with that fuel. We couldn't get anywhere else. Nor can we ask for help . . . even if the radio were working. We're going to pick up these men."

He looked at his crowded audience and a wry smile crossed his face.

"You look so enthusiastic I could almost recommend you all for a medal right away. It's better to make for G beach than sit here and either starve or wait until some passing enemy bomber blasts us out of the water. What do *you* say, Brown?"

Bill Brown sucked deep on his cigarette, shrugged, then said:

"You've never known me disobey an order, sir. If somebody rings down for full speed, half speed, anything, they'll get it if I have the steam."

"And you?" Otis Chambers looked at his twelve-pounder gun crew, then at Slugger Burton. It was Petty Officer Porky Warren who broke the silence which followed, and there was a note of hesitation in his voice when he said:

"I'm a Petty Officer, sir; but I can't navigate. I'm a *guns* man. You tell me what to do and I'll do it. That goes for Big George and Price . . . eh?" and he turned to glare at the shrivelled up Alfie Price.

"Yessir, yessir," Alfie Price would agree with anybody.

Then Slugger Burton spoke.

"I won't say I can navigate, sir. I was sitting for my mate's ticket—in trawlers, of course—when war broke out, and . . ."

"That's settled then." Otis Chambers did not wait to hear any more. "I'll have the cook in here with the charts. You'll man ship. Burton, you'll take the wheel, the other three will help as needed. I'll give you a course in a few minutes. Any questions?"

He seemed to have regained some of his old strength during the interview, though there were lines etched on his forehead— pain lines.

"There's the question of fuel, sir," Bill Brown pointed out. "I dessay we can make this G beach—but what about after?"

"I've never been in the army," Otis Chambers said, "but I've read a lot about wars. I've never known an army in retreat which did not bring some of its stores with it. There'll be oil somewhere along the coast. And listen . . . if we don't do this job, you know what it means . . . a P.O.W. pen for us all. And I don't fancy a German P.O.W. pen, do you? Think about it. Make steam, Brown, and let me know how soon we can get under way."

"You'd think there was nothing wrong with the flipping ship, wouldn't you?" Porky Warren growled, once they were on deck again. "This ain't a ship no more; she's just a floating tin can."

"Well, why didn't you tell him so?" This from Big George. "He asked if there were any questions. Besides, what else can we do, eh? I'm like him, I don't fancy a prisoner of war pen. Not on your flipping nelly. Come on . . . do you want any help, Chiefy?"

Bill Brown pulled a wad of oily cotton waste from his overall pockets and began absent-mindedly wiping his hands, then he grinned and shook his head.

"Maybe you'd best leave the engine-room to them that knows about engines. Thanks all the same. If you could pass the word to old Hodgy that we could do with some chow, that'd be helping. I've got a feeling we've somethin' of a full night in front of us."

Two hours after sunset the *Alice*'s engines came to life again; though for the first hour the best speed they managed was eight knots. Then as they raised the boiler pressure to its normal, they worked up speed to ten knots.

Bill Brown would not offer more. He was saving his fuel oil.

In the wheel-house, which still smelled of charred wood and powder fumes, Slugger and Big George steered. Ahead of them in the velvety dark there were occasional patches of pink—fires, perhaps, in the hills. It could be the Germans shelling villages where troops were still holding out, or the British might be burning stores to keep them out of enemy hands.

Soon the black loom of the land blotted out the starry sky ahead. Then came the part which had Slugger sweating, even though the night was not hot. They rounded Cape Akritas, then began to feel their way along the rugged coastline, looking for the mysterious G beach.

Everything was deadly quiet. No ships were seen. No aircraft hummed overhead. There were no lighthouses to mark the tricky coastline. If ever a ship sailed by guess and by God, it was the *Alice*. At Slugger's suggestion the speed had been cut to five knots, and he was wondering if that might be too much. They were running without riding lights of any kind and every porthole had been blacked out.

He could hear nothing save the soft murmur of the engines and the splash of their bow wave. That they were very close to the coast he knew, for above him and to starboard he could see the blue-black sky dotted with stars. To port everything was just black —dead black with not even a single pin point of light to break the wall of darkness.

Then Alfie Price hissed a warning:

" Sssssssh! Slugger! There's something off the starboard bow. See . . . the flash of water at the bows. It's a Jerry for sure."

Slugger felt gooseflesh creep up the back of his neck and across his cheeks. He, too, could now see the faint splash of phosphorescence sometimes seen at the cut-water of a ship.

He reached out a hand to the engine-room telegraph, meaning to ring down for Bill Brown to stop the engines. But before he could do anything the darkness was gone. Out of the night a searchlight suddenly blazed to life. It was turned full on the *Alice*, dazzling in its brilliance, and sweeping this way and that from stem to stern of the battered vessel.

"Down!" Slugger snarled, and dropped flat to the floor of the wheel-house.

3. Last out from Greece

INSTEAD OF the thunder of guns, however, there came a sharp, commanding voice amplified a dozen times by a ship's loud hailer:

"What are you doing here, you fool?"

"Oh, blimey!" Slugger went limp with relief. He had been certain that this unknown must be a German. He had expected guns to thunder, and the *Alice* to rock under impact of a hail of four-inch shells at point blank range. Unsteadily he got to his feet, cupped his hands about his mouth, and blinking in the glare of the searchlight, gave the challenger the information asked.

"G beach!" A tart voice roared back, "Quarter of a mile farther north. They're waiting for you. I've taken off all I can, but there'll be close on eighty army personnel there. If you are quick I'll wait for you. You look as if you've been in a fight. Are you okay?"

Then Porky Warren stepped forward.

He had suddenly remembered that he was a petty officer, while Slugger was only an A.B. Porky gave his rank, then gave some details of what had happened to them.

"Tell him we're running out of fuel," Slugger prompted. "Ask him if he can help us. We've about half an hour's steaming, that's all."

Porky passed the news over, and there followed a short, grim silence. Then the officer commanding the *Asp*, a Naval corvette, roared back :

"Stay where you are. I'm going to send you some of the troops I've got. Then I'll go back to G beach. I can't give you any fuel, but I'll tow you. That's the best I can do."

For the next forty minutes the corvette's boats plied between the *Asp* and the *Alice*, bringing battle-weary soldiers, many of them slightly wounded. A sub-lieutenant came over and went down to speak to Otis Chambers. When he returned to the deck he spoke to Porky Warren.

"I've just been speaking to your skipper," he said curtly. "He has refused to agree that I take command here. He says someone

The battle-weary soldiers were helped aboard.

called Burton is in command. Is that you?" and he looked at Porky.

"No, sir, him," Porky said stiffly, jerking a thumb towards Slugger.

"I see. All right, Burton; now listen carefully. We are already behind schedule. Once we've got back from G beach, be ready to take a line from us. We'll try and tow you to Crete. One thing you must remember—if we are attacked we shall cast off the tow-line immediately. If we stay together the bombers will get both ships. Understand?"

"Yessir."

"All right, and the best of luck. I'm hoping the bombers will be out after the bigger ships." He acknowledged the salutes of Porky and Slugger, and a minute later he was being rowed back to the *Asp*.

The corvette slid away, back to G beach and the stragglers who had been left there. Slugger left Porky to see to the fifty or more men who had come aboard. Some were armed, many were not. Some were slightly wounded; all were tired and hungry. Old Hodgy got busy in his galley preparing soup and sandwiches.

In the engine-room Slugger spoke to Bill Brown, who had shut down his oil jets and was sitting sucking a dog-end and watching the steam pressure slowly die down in his boilers.

"No chance of getting any oil, Chiefy," Slugger said, flicking his lighter to life and holding it out for Brown to light his stub of cigarette. "What do we do if this corvette leaves us?"

The tubby Yorkshireman sucked at his cigarette for a moment, licked a fragment of tobacco from his lower lip, then shrugged as he said:

"I dunno how much wood there is in the *Alice*, but we could strip what there is and see if it'd burn. There's bound to be a few drums of grease in stores. That'd help the fires . . . but we wouldn't get far. Best thing is to say your prayers and hope the Jerry dive bombers don't find us. If they do . . . them as can swim will last longest."

"Hm!" Slugger pulled absent-mindedly at the lobe of his right ear and went back on deck. There were little groups of soldiers sitting about. None were smoking. They had been warned that even a cigarette in the open might be seen by German troops swarming down to the coast.

It was four o'clock before the *Asp* returned, her decks crowded with the last of the men from G beach. Slugger marvelled at the way the sleek little fighting ship was brought back almost to the exact spot where she had first challenged the *Alice*. She flashed a signal light, and Porky Warren answered it, then a boat was lowered and a light line brought across.

Twenty minutes later the towing hawser had been made fast. The *Asp* paid out some three hundred feet of tow-line, then signalled she was making her end fast and would begin towing.

"You know, you should be here," Slugger said unhappily, as he took the wheel. "I'm supposed to be a technician, not a flippin' helmsman. Petty Officers! Cor, if I . . ."

"You were in trawlers, weren't you?" Porky snapped back. "I'm Armaments. I'm a *fighting* sailor. I . . . look, what are we arguing about? You know all about steering. I don't."

Slugger shrugged and tried to keep the tiny light on the stern of the corvette dead ahead. It was a shaded light, looking more like a tired glow worm than anything else. He had to keep the *Alice* lined up with it. Their speed was four knots. The men aboard the *Asp* hoped to make five when daylight came.

Tired soldiers crowded all available space below decks on the *Alice*, and slept. It was the first real sleep they had had for almost a week. Now that they were aboard ship they felt their troubles were over. The Navy would look after them.

Dawn came in with a stealthy greying of the sky to the east. The black face of the sea gradually turned steely grey. Alfie Price brought a steaming mug of coffee for Slugger and offered to take the wheel for a spell.

Tired and heavy-eyed, Slugger was about to accept the offer when Porky Warren lifted a hand.

" I can't steer, Slugger," he said, " but I'll take the wheel if you are desperate for a rest. Ordinary Seaman Price takes the wheel over my dead body and not before."

" Why don't you gimme a chance?" Alfie

pleaded. " Blimey, Slugger, talk about giving a dog a bad name . . . I makes one or two mistakes soon after I joined the Navy, an' nobody'll gimme a chance to do anything since then."

" If he was playing with paper boats in a bath he'd sink 'em," Porky snarled. " Fetch some sandwiches, Alfie, and don't drop 'em. I never met a man yet who could do so many wrong things in such a short time."

Slugger gulped gratefully. The coffee was hot, strong and sweet. Hodgy knew what tired men needed, and when Alfie Price returned a few minutes later with a plate piled high with thick sandwiches, the bacon between the bread was still warm.

Away to port the coastline of Greece was beginning to show up, and it looked too near to be comfortable. They were cutting across the twenty-five miles of sea which was the mouth of the Gulf of Messinia. For a long time they would be within easy reach of German bombers, and there was nothing they could do but sit tight and hope.

They plugged on, now doing five knots. It was eleven o'clock and Cape Matapan was on the port side when the thing they dreaded happened. A flight of Junkers 87B, the swallow-winged dive-bombers, appeared. They came out from over the Greek coast, heading south.

"I don't wish anybody any harm," Porky Warren muttered, shading his eyes against the sun as he stared upwards, "but I hope they're after bigger game than us. Think they can see us from up there, Slugger?"

"I haven't a clue." Slugger did not take his eyes off the stern of the *Asp*. He was remembering the instructions. If the two ships were attacked the *Asp* would cast off her tow line and the *Alice* would be on her own.

For several minutes all eyes were on the tiny planes flying in perfect formation in a sky of purest blue. The sun occasionally winked on the plastic domes covering pilot and gunner.

"They've not seen us," Porky whispered. "If they . . ."

"Famous last words," Slugger whispered. "Here they come!" But Slugger was wrong. Not all the flight of Junkers peeled off to investigate the tiny ships below. They had more important targets to attack, and only one plane turned off and came down in a long, spiralling dive to take a closer look at the tiny vessels below.

"That's our lot," Slugger said as the tow-line suddenly went slack and the severed end splashed into the sea from the stern of the *Asp*. The corvette's commander was not waiting for the Ju87B to attack. He was moving, and there was a sudden boil of water at the corvette's stern as the engine-room got the command to make all speed.

Those aboard the *Alice* watched in silence. They saw the dive-bomber come out of its easy spiralling descent and straighten into a long dive.

"Strike a light, he's on fire," Alfie Price whispered. "How's that happened?"

"Garn, Alfie, ain't you ever seen no action at all?" Slugger asked. "That's not fire. That's what they call vapour trail. It's made by him coming down so quick. Wish he'd make a mistake an' try and pull out of the dive too late."

The *Asp*, her wake a widening ribbon of

churned-up water, heeled hard as her rudder was put over. It was a piece of splendid anti-cipation, for the Junkers' bomb-aimer had just thumbed his bomb release button. A tiny spot of black screamed down, and threw up a gout of water some fifty yards astern of the *Asp*.

At the same moment, above the angry roar of the Junkers' engine, came the taca-taca-tac—taca-tac of heavy machine guns and the slower drum-beat of a Bofors gun. The bomber flattened out less than a hundred feet from the sea, screamed up to a thousand feet again, then got into position for another attack. The air all around him was pocked with little dark clouds of smoke from the bursting shells.

In real life an asp is a small, venomous serpent, and the corvette was living up to her name. She was spitting death at her attacker, but the pilot of the Junkers earned at least an Iron Cross, Second Class, that morning for his courage and determination.

Down he came again, and though the chase had now moved more than two miles away, those on the motionless *Alice* felt the threat in the snarl of the Junkers' engine as the machine streaked down towards the vessel below.

For twenty minutes the battle went on, the sounds growing fainter and fainter as the *Asp* plunged south-east away from the *Alice* and fought till her gun barrels were too hot to touch.

Three times the Junkers dived on the corvette; twice the plane reappeared, climbing for another attack. After the third time she did not climb into the blue again.

Men with eyes aching from staring across the sunlit water waited and waited.

"They've downed him," someone shouted.

"There should be smoke," someone else pointed out.

"Too far away," another soldier roared. "He's gone straight into the drink . . . probably the pilot bought it and he never pulled out of the dive."

Half a minute passed with everyone staring towards the spot where they had last seen the plane. Then there was a chorus of gasps.

The Junkers had not gone into the sea. He had expended all but one of his bombs, and rather than risk climbing into the air again, a target for the *Asp*'s gunners, he had flattened out at sea level and was now streaking back for base.

The murmur of the Junkers' engine rose to a thrumming, then to a roar, and when she was about half a mile away, and seemed certain to pass the motionless *Alice*, she turned. It was a beautiful piece of flying; dangerous but skilful. The plane's port wing tip was less than six feet from the sea as the pilot banked in a tight turn. Then he flattened out again, and within seconds was thundering towards the *Alice*.

Men cringed and hugged the decks, waiting for the crash and roar of a bomb. Instead, after a few seconds, came the tattoo of bullets raking the ship.

Bullets flattened themselves against the paintwork, stripping it off and leaving gleaming scars on the metal beneath; others tracked a pathway across the sunlit water as the plane swung up to a height of 500 feet to give the gunner his chance. Though he could only fire astern, he made good use of the precious seconds.

The devil drum-beat died away as the Junkers stopped climbing and banked to come in again. On the *Alice* there were some moments of stunned silence. Men who were hugging the scuppers wanted to look up, but were afraid in case the hail of bullets began again. So far, unless someone had died soundlessly, there had been no casualties. There had been no scream of pain; no curse as someone rolled over.

"Here he comes again," a New Zealand sergeant roared, and held his ground for a moment as he watched. The Junkers was being lined up for another run in, this time on a very shallow dive which would take him at mast height over the *Alice*. He had his 550lb. bomb left, and now that he knew the *Alice* had no means of hitting back, he was going to make sure he sank her.

His top speed was 245 miles per hour. He could cruise at 210. He came in now with his flaps down, killing his speed to give him more time to make sure he did not miss.

Through his goggles he could see that the decks of the vessel below were empty. Everyone was keeping out of harm's way.

"Ready, Gunter?" he asked when they were no more than two hundred yards away. "Give them everything when we have passed over. I want to make certain of this one."

Gunter, the rear-gunner, was ready. The pilot dipped his nose a little and moved his gloved thumb over the bomb-release button, his eyes glued to the bomb sights. He had dive-bombed Warsaw, the refugee-crammed roads to Paris and the beaches at Dunkirk. He was an expert. The *Alice* came into his bomb sights.

4. "You gotta be born lucky!"

ON THE *Alice* only a few were watching the Junkers as she came in. One of them was Alfie Price, and there was an odd look on his face, and an even odder gleam in his eyes.

As the approaching plane got within a hundred yards, her engine suddenly screamed louder as the pilot opened the throttle and made ready to lift her out of the dive the moment he had released his bomb. Then Alfie Price moved.

Down on the deck, protected by the low steel bulwarks was a soldier with a machine gun. Alfie suddenly scrambled across and grabbed the gun. He rose, and his eyes widened in sudden terror, for it seemed as if the Junkers 87B was coming straight at him.

He lifted the machine gun, pointed it, and stood there with sudden beads of sweat breaking out over his face while the gun butt bruised his ribs as its muzzle poured nickel-jacketed bullets. Moments later there was a tremendous crash, and the *Alice* shivered

The Junkers 87B was coming straight at him . . .

as the nose of the Junkers snapped off the top six feet of the foremast.

Alfie Price hunched his shoulders and closed his eyes. The gun had stopped its deadly song, for its magazine was empty. Alfie was still hunched when an amazing clamour broke out on the *Alice*. Men were either on their feet or getting up, while away to starboard the Junkers was vanishing beneath the sea.

Instead of sweeping up into a climb the moment the pilot's thumb had squeezed down on the bomb-release, the plane had dipped her nose. Nor had the bomb-release button been depressed. A lucky bullet from Alfie Price's borrowed gun had taken the pilot through the forehead.

No one saw the spat-jacketed landing wheels kick up spray, for what followed took no more than seconds. Two jets of sunlit water spurted into the air as the landing wheels kissed a wavetop, then the Junkers suddenly turned on to her nose as her wheels and struts struck deeper into the sea.

For a second or so the plane was hidden by a tremendous explosion of water. Spray flew in all directions and the brilliant spring sun brought a dozen little rainbows to life in the spray. For perhaps twenty seconds the plane was visible, standing tail up, her shark nose deep in the water, her shallow W wings already beginning to slice deeper into the sea.

Smoke billowed up in her perspex-covered cockpit, blotting out the figure of the gunner as he tried frantically to get out. The plane slid deeper, and then from below the water there was a sudden hollow explosion. The back of the Junkers broke. The tail assembly dropped flat on the sea and lay there for a few moments.

A dirty column of smoke puffed up from the now shattered cockpit, and the gunner had ceased struggling. Men who were scrambling to their feet, not yet fully aware of what had happened, gaped in amazement. Then the plane slid down farther and vanished, dragging with it the tail assembly.

Seconds later there was an explosion from beneath the sea. Whether it was the 550lb. bomb or not, no one will ever know, but a sudden fountain of water was thrown sixty feet into the air—and in it were fragments of the plane.

The men on the *Alice* were too bewildered for a moment to realise their luck. No one really knew what had happened until the man whose bren gun Alfie Price had borrowed, let out a yell. He grabbed Alfie, took the still-smoking gun from his shaking hands, then clapped him on the back with a force which made Alfie gulp and gasp.

"Matey," he roared. "Strike a light! You should have a medal for that. I've never seen anything like it. Here he is; this is the bloke that shot the Jerry down. Borrows my bren gun cool as you like, pops up, gives the Jerry a bellyful just at the right moment— and that was it."

He felt in the breast pocket of his battle dress and a moment later was pressing the remains of a packet of Greek cigarettes into Alfie's still shaking hand.

"Have a gasper, pal. Let 'em all come. If we . . ."

"Hi-ih . . ." It was Slugger from the wheel-house, and he was looking up and to the south. "We're not through yet. They're coming back."

The Junkers which had gone south just over half an hour earlier had reappeared. There had been two flights of four. Now there were six. Whatever they had been attacking must have carried a sting in its tail, for they had lost one, and another, a mile to the rear, was trailing smoke.

The babble of excited comment on the *Alice* died down at sight of the planes. They could not see the black crosses of the wings, but nobody doubted that they were German planes.

In silence soldiers and sailors crowding the *Alice*'s deck space stared and wondered. Slugger turned to Porky and said :

"But for that smoke I'll bet they wouldn't have noticed us. Pity the durned thing blew up."

Porky nodded, and winced a moment later as one of the planes peeled off and began to dive down towards the *Alice*. It was coming either to see what had happened or to finish off this impudent little craft.

The soldier whose bren gun Alfie Price had borrowed, suddenly turned to him and, thrusting the gun back into his hands, said:

"Here you are, chum. A chance to make it two. Wait a tick . . . I'll put another magazine in. It's my last . . . but you're welcome. Get him on the nose like . . ." And there he stopped, for Alfie, his face a pasty cream colour, was trying to push the warm bren gun back into its owner's grasp.

"You do it, I've done one," he gabbled.

"Me! I wouldn't have the nerve to stand up to one like you did. Here . . . come on, he'll be on to us in a tick. You got the other easy as pie."

"No, you gotta be born lucky to do it twice," Alfie stuttered. "I'm not lucky. Ask anybody on the *Alice*. I'm the unluckiest bloke in the Navy . . . bar none," and turning, he ran to the bridge steps and joined Slugger and Porky in the wheel-house.

The air was thrilling now to the scream of the Junkers' Jumo engine. She looked as if she really meant to dive straight on to the crowded deck space of the crippled *Alice*.

Suddenly a blue-eyed, sun-burned New

Zealander lifted his gun, at the same time yelling:

"Come on, lads . . . I'm hanged if I'm going to stand and be shot down like a crippled sheep. Come on . . . all together. Somebody's bound to hit something," and he began to shoot.

Others followed his example. These men, dirty, bedraggled, and weary after a fighting retreat, were not rookies. They had been toughened in battle and they rallied to the call.

If the Junkers' pilot had had even one bomb left the story might have ended differently; but all bombs and ammunition for the machine guns in the wings had gone in an attack on a transport the night before. Nor could the Junkers' rear-gunner do anything until they had passed over the *Alice*.

With bullets thudding into his engine cowling the German suddenly decided to turn away. He banked at a speed which made his plane quiver, and as he did so a bullet cut an oil line.

For thirty seconds nothing seemed wrong. He completed his bank, but instead of starting to climb back after his comrades, he levelled out and headed for Cape Matapan. Smoke was beginning to pour from his engine—smoke which thickened and suddenly grew dramatically thinner for a moment or so as the escaping oil ignited.

Then over the air, unheard by the men on the *Alice*, came a call for help from the pilot to the rest of his squadron.

"*Achtung! Achtung!* I am going down with my engine on fire. That ship is a Britisher and crammed with troops. She is a decoy. Bombing should be from a height. The vessel is well-armed. I . . ." and that was as far as he got, for suddenly there was a sea of flame all around him in the cockpit itself. He unhooked the hood and a second or so later he and his rear-gunner were bailing out. Their blazing plane roared onwards for another thirty seconds, losing height all the time, then it plunged into the sea.

One man on the *Alice* was not cheering when the news reached him that a second plane was down. Otis Chambers yelled until Hodge, the cook, came to see what was wrong.

"Shot another Jerry down, sir," he announced, his eyes blazing with triumph. "He was coming . . ."

"Send Able Seaman Burton to me," Otis Chambers snapped, "and I want him at the double."

It took Hodge a minute or more to get to Slugger, and another two minutes before Slugger could get through the press of excited men to his skipper's cabin. Otis Chambers wasted no time.

"Burton, you've got to get this ship away from here. At once. Don't start telling me you have no fuel oil. I know that. Rip every bit of woodwork out of the ship . . . take my bunk if you need it. Tell Chief Engineer Brown that you have got to get to the coast inside an hour . . . in less time if you can."

"The coast, sir!" Slugger's eyes goggled at the idea. "We're hardly clear of Greece, sir. Cape Matapan's on the port side and . . ."

"I may be injured, Burton, but I can see through the porthole, and I'm still capable of thinking. You can't get to Crete, so get as near the Greek coast as you can.

Don't ask me why; I'll tell you. You can't knock down two German bombers and expect to get away with it. Jerry's got his tail up at the moment, and as soon as they know on the mainland that a tuppence-half-penny ship out here has had the cheek to shoot down a couple of Junkers, they'll be out after our blood. I don't want to be blasted out of my bunk by a Jerry bomb. Now . . . tell the chief engineer what I've said, and get that noisy rabble on deck tearing the woodwork out of this ship. She'll have to burn wood when the fuel oil is finished."

Slugger looked like a punch-drunk boxer when he hurried out on deck again. Lieutenant Otis Chambers obviously did not expect the *Asp* to return to tow them to safety —though what they could hope for if they headed for the Greek coast he just did not know.

He hurried down to the engine-room and reported to Bill Brown. All the Yorkshireman did was shrug. He felt for the cigarette end he usually kept behind his ear, sighed when he found nothing, then said :

"I came to the *Alice* in '39 when she was taken over by the Navy, and Otis Chambers was given command of her. It doesn't pay to argue with him, Slugger. If he gives an order—obey it. He knows what he's doing."

Slugger was still unhappy when he returned to the deck to ask the soldiers to start stripping the ship of what little woodwork was left. He told them they needed it for raising steam, and there was no lack of enthusiasm. When a sixty pound head of steam pressure had been built up, Chief Engineer Brown signalled that he was ready to move.

Very slowly the *Alice* got under way and swung round until her bows were pointing towards Cape Matapan.

"There's trouble brewing, Slugger," Petty Officer Warren murmured as he came up into the battered wheel-house. "What are you going to tell 'em when they ask where we're going?"

"I'll tell them to mind their own flippin' business," Slugger said tartly. "I'm obeying orders, and they're only passengers anyway."

Five minutes later a corporal of the 174

Light Ack-Ack scrambled up into the wheel-house. He was met by a cold-eyed Slugger who jerked an imperious thumb at him and snapped:

"Get off the bridge, mister. We've enough to do without passengers getting in the way."

The corporal's eyes hardened, but he did not back an inch.

"Listen, matey," he said angrily, "we were on a real ship—the *Asp*, until you came on the scene. We didn't ask to be transferred to this wreck. All we want to know is where you are taking us. We may not be sailors, but some of us think you shouldn't be heading towards the coast. What's the idea?"

"I'm obeying orders," Slugger said, his voice as coldly angry as the corporal's.

"If you're taking us back to Greece, you've got another think coming," the corporal snarled. "Are you going to turn this ship round? We want to go south, for Crete, or Egypt; *we are not going back to Greece*."

"I've got my orders," Slugger said stiffly. "And in the Navy we obey orders. Now get . . ." The corporal made a rush. Porky Warren tried to stop him and got a fistful of hard knuckles for his reward. He reeled back, clapping a hand to a burst lower lip.

Slugger Burton turned like a tiger, and the left hook which had earned him the boxing championship even before he had shaken properly into Navy uniform, took the corporal flush on the jaw. The punch was a short one but the power behind it must have been like a miniature steam hammer.

The corporal's head jerked back, and a moment later he was falling backwards. He would have fallen out of the wheel-house and down to the deck if Slugger had not grabbed him. As it was, he was able to ease him down the six-runged ladder to the waiting group of taut-faced soldiers.

They grabbed the corporal and heaved him gently to one side. Then a big Australian grabbed the ladder rail. He stopped when Slugger slid down the steps and pushed him back.

Slugger was breathing hard as he faced the ring of angry soldiers.

"You don't want to go our way, eh?" he snarled, his eyes like ice.

"We're not going back to Greece," the Australian yelled. "Listen, cobber, if you are not prepared to try and get away—we are."

"Okay," Slugger stepped to one side, looked up as Porky Warren, one hand held to his bruised mouth, put a foot on the top rung of the ladder, and said: "Come on, Porky. We've got a new crew. I'll just nip down to the engine-room and tell the chief engineer that he can hand over to the Army."

A hand grabbed him by the shoulders and spun him round. The Australian was at least five inches taller than Slugger and built like an ox. Slugger hit him in the solar plexus. As the man started to double up, he cracked him on the side of the jaw. It was a clean K.O., Slugger's best yet, and the Aussie sagged to the deck.

"They do say," Slugger snapped, "that the bigger they are the harder they fall. Now, who's next?"

The ring had widened. One man reached

The punch took him full on the jaw.

back for a bren gun leaning against the scuppers; but he stopped when Slugger said more quietly :

" Look, I am not arguing. You can take over the wheel-house, and you can take over the engine-room . . . but unless you've got someone who can steer and someone who can run the engines, you haven't the chance of a paper cat in a burning barn. If you'll take my advice you'll have another meeting. I'll tell you one thing . . . I'm not looking for a cushy number in a German P.O.W. camp. I'll give you five minutes to make up your minds whether you want to take over or whether you'll trust the Navy to handle the run."

Then he turned and strode along the deck to the cook's galley. Porky Warren followed him and the *Alice*, gradually working up to a speed of five knots, trundled on towards Matapan with no one at the wheel.

5. "We'll have oil or bust!"

"ARE YOU GOING to tell the Skipper?" Porky asked when he joined Slugger in the galley.

"He's got enough to worry about," Slugger said soberly. "Where's the sugar, Hodgy? Yeah ... two spoonfuls. Ta." And he stirred his coffee briskly, then reached for a biscuit.

"Here, here," Hodge warned. "You may have been put in the wheel-house, Slugger, but to me you are still just a ruddy A.B. Don't come any of the Skipper's tricks. You're not the boss till you get the flipping rings round your cuffs."

"Eat, drink and be merry," Slugger said, suddenly smiling. "We don't know what we'll be doing to-morrow. We ... hello, hello, looks like a deputation from the passengers."

Two men were standing outside the cook's galley—a New Zealand sergeant and a private wearing the badges of the Black Watch. When Slugger stepped out on deck the sergeant said:

"Look, matey, none of us want to be taken prisoner. You convince me that you are not planning to surrender the ship, and . . ."

"You're the first fellow I've heard use the word *surrender*," Slugger broke in on the sergeant. "The idea is that if we head towards the coast it will look as if we may be thinking of surrendering. The skipper is sure we'll have German bombers out after us pretty soon. If we head south-east towards Crete they'll bomb the living daylights out of us. They won't if we're heading towards Greece."

"That makes sense," the two soldiers agreed. "But we are bound to reach land . . . what then?"

"Well, we need oil," Slugger said. "If we can find a small port and get some fuel oil, we'll make a dash for it during the night."

New Zealander and Black Watch private

exchanged quick glances. The New Zealander nodded.

"Okay, we'll back you. It'll mean a party going ashore. I'll find out who's fit, and what weapons we have. Can you fix up a decent meal for us so we don't go ashore with empty bellies?"

"Hear that, Hodgy?" Slugger turned to the galley, and Hodge, wiping out one of the coffee cups, nodded.

"Yeah, corn beef hash . . . but there'll be plenty of it, and real coffee. Can't do more."

"That'll do fine," the Black Watch private said, suddenly grinning. "Come on, Sarge. We've some hard talking to do. Some of the lads aren't pleased with the direction we're taking."

Fifteen minutes later the wisdom of heading north instead of towards Crete was borne out. A flight of three Junkers 87B dive-bombers came out from north of Cape Matapan, climbing rapidly. Slugger was back in the wheel-house again, and he had posted Big George and Alfie Price in the bows with glasses.

They gave the alarm, and at once Slugger nodded to Porky who, grabbing a portable loud hailer, stepped to the bridge-wing and yelled:

"Out of sight, everybody . . . and no shooting. No shooting, do you hear? Get out of sight and don't attempt to shoot."

The bombers were obviously looking for the *Alice*, but when they were still a mile from her the three planes stopped climbing, and after a moment one put its nose down in a dive.

"Keep your fingers crossed, Slugger," Porky Warren said tensely. "These blokes are usually red hot at this game. If he means to bomb us, we'll be swimming for home any minute."

In the bows Big George and Alfie were huddled under the twelve-pounder gun. There was not a man on the *Alice*'s decks. Slugger stepped as far back from the wheel as possible so that he could watch the dive-bomber approach simply by staring up through the gap where the wheel-house roof should have been.

It was a frightening sight. It seemed to

suggest that the pilot had his plane lined up on the *Alice*'s wheel-house.

"Well, drop 'em, drop 'em," Porky pleaded, and did not know he was speaking. Both he and Slugger were waiting for the first sign of small black objects falling from the dive bomber.

The roar of the Jumo engine grew almost unbearable. In the last second or so the dive-bomber's speed seemed to multiply. The silhouette became solid, and with a deafening scream the plane zipped over the top of the *Alice*. She was so low that if anyone had had the nerve to look up they would have seen that the bomb bay racks under the wings were full. One single shot from the *Alice* would have invited certain attack.

As the thunderous roar of the engines began to fade, Slugger and Porky opened their eyes. Porky had the first and second fingers of both hands crossed and he grinned weakly as he caught Slugger's gaze on them.

"I've got a feeling I'd better keep 'em crossed till we get back to a British port. Think they'll come down again?"

Slugger could only shrug and watch the

planes. The one which had dived on them was climbing fast to join the other two who were cruising in a wide circle. They had certainly come out to look for the impudent little vessel which had so ruthlessly disposed of two of their planes.

" I'll tell you this, Slugger, old Otis knows a thing or two," Porky said. " If we hadn't been steaming towards Greece . . . wuff, wuff, and it'd have been a case of 'The Admiralty regrets . . .' eh?"

Slugger nodded. He was waiting for the planes to turn and head back for land, but they continued to circle for nearly an hour, by which time the *Alice* was within a mile of Cape Matapan.

It was then one o'clock—a full six hours before sunset. Slugger turned the *Alice* north-east, and at a mere two knots they crawled parallel to the coast. They were about 80 miles from the north-west tip of Crete, a trip they could have accomplished in seven hours if they had had fuel.

Twice more during the afternoon they saw flights of German bombers go over and guessed that the fleet of ships, large and small, which had been evacuating the army from Greece, would soon hear the whistle of falling bombs.

The *Alice* presented a sorry spectacle, for the soldiers had stripped her of every last stick of timber which could be used in the boiler fires. Down below Bill Brown and his " black " gang were swearing and sweating as they tried to keep a reasonable head of steam, by burning wood in fireboxes equipped for burning atomised fuel oil. It was not easy, and tempers were badly frayed by the time the sun set.

In mid-afternoon there had been a council of war in Otis Chambers's cabin with Slugger, Porky, the New Zealand sergeant and the Black Watch private. To Slugger's amazement, Otis Chambers gave them all a drink from his private store.

" I'm sorry I shan't be able to come ashore with you," he said, when they were all smoking his cigarettes. " But with a leg temporarily out of action I'd only be a nuisance. However, I have been studying a chart of the coastline. There are several villages. They are small, but you could be lucky and maybe find one without a German patrol keeping an eye on things. Burton there," and he pointed at Slugger, " will take you in as soon as it is dark ... and the rest is in the hands of you Army gentlemen. I'm sure you'll be able to cope. Any questions or comments?"

The New Zealander drew in a long, deep breath, then finishing his drink at a gulp, said :

" Sir, we have seven really fit men available. All other ranks are nursing wounds of one kind or another. I'll have to ask you to detail some of your crew to come with us. Seven or eight would make up a nice handy party. We'll need someone to give us covering fire if there are any Germans in the place, while the rest look for oil."

" Seven or eight, eh? Hm! Able Seaman Burton will be able to tell you more precisely than I can, how many men we have available. How many, Burton?"

" We could take two from the engine-room and there's Petty Officer Warren, myself, Price, Big George, Hodge."

" You can't take Hodge," Chambers said

promptly. "He has our wounded to care for, and he's needed in the galley. So that means six, Sergeant. Will that do?"

The New Zealander pondered for a moment, then with a slightly sheepish grin said:

"I'd rather have five or seven men from the ship, sir, if you don't mind. I have seven. If six seamen come, that'll make thirteen. I'm not normally superstitious, but it happens to be Friday. Thirteen men landing on a Friday is a bit too much. We need a lot of luck, and I don't mean bad luck."

"We could leave Seaman Price aboard, sir," Porky Warren suggested, and with a grin which he hoped would explain a lot of things added: "You know what he's like, sir."

"Do I?" Otis Chambers asked quietly. "If I remember aright, he shot down the first Junkers dive-bomber, didn't he? I wouldn't write him off completely, Warren. What do you say, Burton?"

"If we're to leave anybody, Price would be my choice, sir."

"All right, Price it is."

Arms and ammunition for the shore party

were collected, examined, cleaned and doled out. There were two bren guns with five magazines of ammunition between them. Several pistols, two Mark I Lee-Enfield rifles, with fifty rounds of ammunition, and three hand grenades.

An hour from sunset Slugger went below to consult again with Otis Chambers. He fixed their position by the bluff headland of Matapan, and was shown the tiny fishing village which Chambers thought they should raid. It was about three miles from their present position.

"You have everything arranged, Burton?" Otis Chambers asked, and when Slugger nodded, the older man said quietly: "Then go in now, before it gets too dark. You can't hope to find your way in without a pilot once the light has gone."

"Go in by daylight, sir?" Slugger wondered if he was hearing aright.

"Go in now. If you are flying an Ensign, take it down. Go in as if you were going into a home port. The chances are there won't be any Germans there anyway. If there are, they won't fire on you. They'll never suspect what you are up to. Possibly they'll think you are coming in to surrender. I've no doubt units on the coast have been warned—the Germans didn't let us off the hook this noon just because they like it. It was because we were heading towards the Greek coast and not away from it. Barefaced cheek, Burton, wins many a victory. If you try creeping in after dark you could run aground, or have the alarm raised by some frightened sentry."

"Aye-aye, sir," Slugger went out, trying to tell himself that he was not dreaming. He hurried down to the engine-room and warned Bill Brown that they were to go in as the sun was setting. The Yorkshireman nodded, spat towards his boilers where the last pile of wood from the ship's bunks was crackling away, and said :

"We'll just about manage it. As soon as you tie up I'll clear out under the boilers and get my oil jets into position again. The best of luck, Slugger, and if you don't get any oil, I hope we'll meet up in a fairly decent prisoner-of-war camp," and he winked.

Slugger did not feel like winking back.

Prisoner-of-war camp! The words sent a shiver through him as he hurried back on deck to warn the New Zealand sergeant that they were going in—now, not after darkness had fallen.

A minute or so later the *Alice* was heading for the coast and a tiny inlet which housed a fishing village.

He found the entrance to the inlet without trouble and was glad the hills shut off the red light of the setting sun. It seemed almost gloomy in this miniature fjord whose rocky walls rose several hundred feet, and whose waters were as placid as those of a lake.

They turned a slight bend and there was the village—no more than two hundred yards ahead. The houses were on a gentle slope, the upper reaches of which were still pink-lit by the last rays of the sun.

"Oh-ho, see that!" Porky Warren exclaimed. "Waiting for us on the quay itself. Did that New Zealander say he wanted all the good luck that was going? There's no good luck here."

For a moment Slugger's hand strayed

*The Germans stared at the approaching
ship . . .*

towards the engine-room telegraph, then came away. There was no point in stopping the engines now. They had been seen just as surely as they could see the German soldiers on the rickety wooden quay. Otis Chambers had suggested that the Germans might not yet have reached these isolated fishing villages; but for once he had been wrong.

There was a lorry on the quay, and German soldiers were unloading what looked like oil drums. At sight of the *Alice* work stopped. The men stared at the approaching ship but no one moved to reach for a weapon.

"Well?" Porky Warren asked tautly.

"We're going in," Slugger said. "We can't turn back now, anyway. Are our lot ready?" He jerked a thumb to the scuppers where the landing party was crouching out of sight.

"They're ready!" Porky answered, and wiped tiny beads of sweat from his lip.

"Okay. We said we'd get oil—or bust, and this is it. I hope we don't—bust, that's all." He swung the engine-room telegraph over to " Stand by ", then braced himself as the *Alice* glided quietly on and the men by the lorry moved towards the edge of the quay. If there was shooting, Slugger had no cover.

6. So near to success

SLUGGER rang down for "Slow astern" so that he could swing the *Alice*'s starboard against the quay; the soft murmur of the engines seemed loud in the quietness. In the fading light the Germans had not realised that this was an enemy ship. With the British concentrating all their efforts on pulling their army out of Greece, it would have been ludicrous for a small ship like this to come in. One German called something to Slugger whom he could see peering along the starboard. Bringing a vessel alongside was not easy and Slugger was sweating.

The wooden quay shuddered a little as the *Alice* drove her bows obliquely into the old timbering. A moment later it seemed as if the ship was raining bodies. The New Zealand sergeant was first over, his friend from the Black Watch was at his heels, and the rest of them followed, with Porky Warren last. Slugger was still at the wheel, his hand automatically flipping the engine-room tele-graph lever over once more to " Stand by ".

Two shots were fired. One by a German, one by the New Zealander. The German who fired went down and never got up again. The New Zealander was a profes-sional soldier and he did not waste ammuni-tion.

Within seconds the dazed Germans were lined up against their lorry, their hands high, while a soldier whipped off their webbing, tossing it towards the ship with the remark that the ammunition might come in useful.

Two soldiers raced to each end of the quay, guns at the ready. The rest of the raiders were already rolling part of the lorry's load towards the ship. Luck was with them, for the lorry had been unloading diesel fuel. Several motor boats were coming in the next day to begin a search of the beaches for British stragglers. They would need re-fuelling.

The men still aboard the *Alice* had been told what they were to do if oil were found. They had ropes ready, and soon the first fifty-gallon drum was banging and clanking against the bullet- and shell-scarred side of the *Alice*.

The second drum was on its way when the firing broke out. There was a warning yell from one end of the quay, then the quick rat-at-tat-tat of a bren. That burst of fire was answered by two single shots—then there was silence.

The man who had fired called a warning in the direction of the ship:

"Better be quick. I didn't get the chap . . . and he's got away. There'll be more coming."

The New Zealand sergeant took command on the quay. He put two men in charge of the Germans and they were forced to roll the oil drums to the edge of the quay, ready for loading. The men were front-line troops, but they offered no resistance. There was something about the rag-tag-and-bobtail gang of raiders which would have made even the bravest man hesitate to defy them.

On the *Alice*, Slugger and the engine-room gang hustled the first drum down below. Bill Brown unscrewed the cap immediately. He had just connected the drum to his oil feed with a makeshift pipe when there was a sudden burst of bren gun fire from the quay.

"Get the other drums down," the Yorkshireman ordered. "I'll flash-up the fires. This is going to be touch-and-go, and if we don't *go* quickly we'll *touch* out for a prison camp."

His second-in-command and the two stokers tore back on deck. There was firing at the north end of the quay, and in the fading light the flashes from a bren gun revealed two khaki-clad soldiers flat on the quay, firing at something unseen beyond the first of the houses.

Then came a louder *wump*. There was a faint scream as a shell vanished into the dusk, and for a second or so there was silence—a silence broken by the ominous thrum-thrum-thrum of engines. One of the men at the north end of the quay swivelled round, still lying flat. He cupped his hands about his mouth and roared:

"Get moving . . . GET MOVING! They've got a tank. We'll try and hold it."

Slugger recognised the voice. It was the

New Zealander. The fourth drum of oil was being hefted aboard, and as the unseen tank fired again Slugger decided to take the New Zealand sergeant's advice.

"Back everybody," he yelled. "Everybody aboard. We'll try and get away." As he spoke there was a savage blast of machine-gun fire from the unseen tank, and bullets ricochetted into the gloom after striking the quay planking. For the moment it looked as if the tank crew could not depress their guns enough to get at the two men holding them up.

Then, as the men on the quay got the fourth oil drum aboard and began to scramble over the *Alice*'s stern, there came the sharp crack of an exploding grenade. Out of the corner of his eye Slugger saw the splash of fire. He saw something else— one of the two men down there, and he could not tell whether it was the New Zealand sergeant or the Black Watch private, half-rose and then flopped down again.

Swinging the engine-room telegraph over to "Slow ahead", Slugger started the steam steering. It was going to be tricky work getting the *Alice* away from this quay. The narrow inlet, like a miniature Norwegian fjord, was barely wide enough for a vessel like the *Alice* to swing round in. Yet swing round he must.

There was more machine-gun fire, followed by the savage crump of the tank's 75mm. gun. He heard the New Zealand sergeant yelling for the men on the *Alice* to give him covering fire and Slugger leaped across to the port wing of the bridge to see what was happening. The *Alice* was already beginning to move, swinging gently with her stern grinding against the rotting timbers of the old quay.

In the few minutes since they had arrived, night seemed to have fallen like a cloak, and above them the stars were beginning to show in a darkening sky. From the port rail every man with a weapon was blazing away at the spot where they thought the tank would be.

Then the darkness was swept away as twin beams of light, which in the gloom seemed as brilliant as the most powerful searchlights. The Germans had driven a car on to the south end of the quay and switched on its headlamps.

There was a sudden chorus of encouraging yells from the men on the *Alice* to the New Zealander who was staggering along the quay with the wounded Black Watch private slung like a sack over one shoulder.

"Put the lights out, somebody!" The bellowed command brought the soldiers to their senses, and within seconds the night was alive with the crackle of rifle and pistol fire. One car headlamp was shot out immediately, but the other continued to light up the whole length of the quay.

In the wheel-house Slugger Burton was chewing anxiously at his lower lip, his hand over the engine-room telegraph lever. The *Alice* seemed suddenly to have begun to move more quickly. She was edged round, and the vibration as her stern ground against the quay was dying down. In seconds now, unless he ordered Bill Brown to stop the engines, they would be on their way.

"Hurry!" he roared, his voice cracked with anxiety. "HURRY!"

A moment later, looking like some monster from a forgotten age, the tank nosed out of the gloom on to the quay, to be lit up at once by the single headlamp.

Tactac-tac-a-taca-taca-taca!

The machine-gun chattered angrily. Bullets struck sparks from the stern of the *Alice* and forced the men there to duck for safety behind the iron bulwarks. The New Zealander stumbled, went down, got to his feet again, then sprawled full length once more.

The mixed crowd of soldiers in the stern of the *Alice* blasted at the tank with every weapon they had, but it had no more effect than if they had been shelling it with peas. The bullets struck sparks from the armoured plating, but like a huge, ugly animal, it remained there, and again its machine-gun poured a devastating stream of bullets at the *Alice*.

They smashed themselves out of shape and whined off into the night. One droned through the wheel-house, coming in at the door and out where the window had long since been shattered. Slugger ducked *after* the droning, but the bullet was already far away.

He looked back and felt sick. They were away from the quay now. There was a widening gap between their stern and that headlamp-lit stretch of planking on which lay the New Zealand sergeant and the wounded Black Watch private. The two men who had given the *Alice* its chance to get away were being left behind.

Wump! There was a muffled flash from the tank's gun, and the shell screamed over the wheel-house and cracked with frightening force against the rocky side of the fjord.

Then, with a sudden roaring of its engine, the car whose headlamp had been so useful to the tank, was slowly turned so that the single beam now shone on the *Alice* as she tried to get away. Thus lit up she was a sitting duck to the tank gunner.

At such close range even her shells would smash through the ship's plates with ease. Two or three hits in the stern would smash the rudder mechanism, and that would be that.

"Put the light out," Slugger screamed again, and from the deck below came an angry:

"Come down and have a go yourself, matey, and see how long you last."

The men down there had reason to be annoyed with Slugger. Not only was the tank machine gunner spraying the *Alice* with bullets, but someone near the car was also firing.

The noise was ear-splitting—a devilish tattoo. Then from behind Slugger came a panting voice:

"All right, Burton . . . I'll take over."

Slugger turned in shocked amazement. Behind him, dimly seen in the reflected light from the nearby quay, was Otis Chambers. Behind him, and helping him, were the two stokers. They had brought Lieutenant Chambers up on the starboard side where there was least danger, and had literally hoisted him to the bridge.

Slugger just stood and stared as Otis Chambers hopped to the wheel. The man who had commanded the *Alice* from the day she had been taken into the Navy made an odd picture. His head was still swathed in bandages, and there was still a piece of stout board from his ankle to his armpit, held in place with strips of a bed sheet.

He was just about the last man to take command of a ship in a tight corner like this, and Slugger was so petrified he simply stood and stared, unable to think, unable to speak.

He watched Otis Chambers push over the engine-room telegraph to "Slow astern", watched him spin the steering wheel, then he jumped as the pale-faced commander suddenly snapped:

"Now, Burton, set some of the depth-charges for explosion at minimum depth. Fire them the moment you hear me shout."

"Aye, aye, sir." Eighteen months of obeying commands without question helped Slugger to reply, and helped him to get out of the wheel-house. He was going first of all to the port side, but Otis Chambers stopped him.

"Don't be a fool, Burton. Go that way and you'll have your head shot off before you can say 'chips'. Port side, and hurry."

Slugger almost fell down the ladder to the deck. The two stokers were there, and one of them whispered:

"He's mad. What the heck's he think he's doing?"

Slugger did not stay to answer, for from the wheel-house, almost as if the skipper had heard the whispered comment, had come a rasping command for Slugger to get a move on.

For the first time in his life Slugger realised what it was like to be a soldier. In the *Alice* there had been danger—they had escorted hundreds of ships, and attacked a number of submarines. They had also been under fire several times, but it had always been shell-fire.

The chatter of innumerable bullets striking the *Alice*, the flashes of the tank's machine gun, and the rather slow, but frightening *wump* of the large gun all added up to a terrifying experience. Slugger felt as if he were the only one aboard, and the one man against whom all the fire was directed.

As he set the first of the depth-charges he was continually ducking and blinking. It seemed utterly mad to do what Otis Chambers was doing. The *Alice* was now slowly beginning to back towards the quay and was presenting an even larger target than before.

A tank shell crashed into the stern, exploded somewhere inside, and the deck under Slugger's feet seemed to lift. Then, above the welter of sound came the command:

" Fire !"

Slugger had only set two depth-charges, but he obeyed automatically. Down went the lever, there was a sudden rushing roar, and first one, then the second depth-charge was swept into the air.

The tank gun roared again. The shell ripped into the funnel, and there was a tremendous roar as it exploded. Red hot metal shot up the funnel like overgrown sparks from a railway train's smokestack. The funnel trembled and sagged sideways like a drunken man.

Then the depth-charges hit the water beside the quay.

The water was very deep, and the two canisters went down and out of sight with no more than a sinister plop-plop !

The tank's gun roared again . . .

As the *Alice* began to surge away from the quay the tank hatch was pushed up and a German looked out then yelled something to a companion inside.

Within seconds the tank's gun roared again and the machine-gun began its terrifying taca-taca-taca-taca-tac, the bullets striking sparks in a score of places and producing a metallic hammering which made Slugger wince.

Then, deep down, the depth-charges exploded. Trawlers are made to ride the seas like ducks, and the men who built the *Alice* would have been proud of their handiwork had they seen the vessel's behaviour during the next minute or so.

Out of the black depth a mighty mountain of foam-lashed water reared up, its peak a hundred feet above the quay. With it came a momentary orange glow from the undersea explosion.

Slugger felt the stern of the *Alice* lift. In sudden wild fear he rose, meaning to get farther along the port side where he might find some protection.

Even as he rose he was picked up like a

shrivelled autumn leaf and carried over the side. The *Alice* survived because she had her stern to the mountain of water which blasted up from the depths just in front of the ricketty old quay. The trawler rolled as if she would turn turtle. Water crashed on to her stern, then sluiced over the rails as she rolled from side to side.

Waves chased one another wildly out in the direction of the sea. Slugger Burton, dazed, and half-choked with salt water, was carried by the waves to the far end of the quay and dropped on to the shingle. He heaved his head off the stones as another wave came in to wash him up even higher. Feebly he struggled on for a few yards then flopped face down.

7. One man left ashore

ON THE *Alice* Otis Chambers had been prepared for the aftermath of the two depth-charges. He had lowered himself to the wheel-house floor the moment he gave the firing order, and he was lying there when the blast struck the ship.

With the *Alice* still rocking like a toy boat, Chambers heaved himself upright. It was not easy, for his injured leg was held stiff as an iron bar by the splint.

He pushed the engine-room telegraph lever over to " Hard astern ", then when he was answered, eased it over to " Stand by ".

On the quay there was a scene of terror. The tank had been thrown over and was now upside down. The car at the end of the quay was still in position and its one headlight still lit the scene. The men who had been firing from behind it had gone. The lorry with the oil drums had been pushed back a dozen yards, but was still upright.

Otis Chambers stared towards the quay for a moment. The mighty upthrusting flood of water had buckled the rotten planking in all directions yet they had to put some men ashore. He yelled for the crew and kept on yelling until men began to appear from below. Many of them were bleeding and all were bruised. The wild gyrations of the *Alice* had thrown them about like peas in a drum.

One or two men still clung to their weapons. Otis glared at them as if trying to decide whether or not they were fit for the job.

"I want a party ashore," he yelled. "Quick, pick up our two men, and if you can get another drum of oil aboard . . . so much the better."

A score of pairs of eyes turned in his direction. Most of the soldiers had never seen him before, for he had been lying in his bunk when they had been transferred from the *Asp* to the *Alice*.

"Shake a leg . . . shake a leg," Chambers bellowed. "This isn't a half-day picnic. Get a move on. Who's in command? Burton

". . . BURTON! Where's Burton?" he roared as a pale-faced Petty Officer Porky Warren came forward.

"Don't know, sir."

"Well, send him to me when you find him," Chambers snapped. "If any more tanks arrive—hold 'em off, so that the rest of the men can get back aboard."

"Aye, aye, sir." Porky was dazed by the events of the past minute or so, but if Otis Chambers had told him to stand on his head on the quay he would have done it. There was something about this pale-faced man with the bandaged head which made men obey without question.

Within twenty seconds men were scrambling over the stern. Some went to pick up the New Zealander and the Black Watch man. Others hurried to retrieve one of the fifty-gallon drums of oil. One or two had been lifted into the sea by the blast; others had simply rolled along the quay.

In addition to the light from the headlamp of the car at the end of the quay there was a new light. A fire had started just off the waterfront and the flames were spreading.

By this light the injured men and one drum of oil were brought aboard.

"All back?" Chambers cried, when it seemed as if the last man had left the quay.

"Yessir," Porky Warren was recovering his nerve. There had been no sign of further activity from the Germans. It was beginning to look as if only a single tank and perhaps two lorry loads of troops had come here, bringing oil to re-fuel the fast motor launches expected the next day. With luck the *Alice* might still get out to sea . . . and freedom.

"All right. Get the injured below. Warren, tell the men to stand by. We're not out of this tight corner yet."

"Aye, aye, sir."

Otis Chambers took a last look along the port side of the *Alice*, red lit by the fires ashore, then he pushed the engine-room telegraph over to "Slow ahead". When the pulse of the engines made itself felt through the wheel-house boards under his feet, he blew down the voice pipe—the ordinary telephone to the engine-room had been out of action since the wheel-house roof was blown off.

When Bill Brown, the chief engineer, answered him, Otis said:

"We are on our way, Mr. Brown. I've got you another drum of oil . . . and if you don't get me to Crete I'll have the skin off your back."

"After to-night, nothing is impossible, sir," Brown replied, and there was a tired chuckle in his voice. Like every other man on the *Alice* he had been on duty without a break for over 24 hours and the strain was beginning to tell.

Her growing wake illuminated by the fire she was leaving behind, the *Alice* began to work up speed. Bill Brown could not be extravagant, so she would not do more than seven knots—but she was on her way.

On shore Slugger Burton was coming round. He felt sick with the salt water he had swallowed, and his head was aching. When he lifted a hand to the lump just above his forehead he whistled in dismay. In the light of the fire he could see blood on his hand. That helped to bring him to his senses even quicker.

He sat up and looked about him. The fire in the houses behind the quay drew his attention first. Then he saw something moving on the seaward side. The shape was becoming indistinct, but after a moment, with horror growing in his heart, he staggered to his feet.

"Hi ... Hi ..." he gave a croaking cry and waved desperately. "Wait ... WAIT!"

The *Alice* was slipping away. She was leaving him behind.

Slugger looked round. His first thought was to run along the side of the fjord to the headland and perhaps swim out to the *Alice*, or make himself heard by someone on board as she was passing. He dropped the idea at once. This tiny fishing village was situated at the head of a narrow inlet, and the walls rose a hundred feet or more, sheer from the water. By the time Slugger had climbed up to the top the *Alice* would be at sea.

He sat down, felt in his jumper pocket for a cigarette and brought out a sodden packet. He looked at it in disgust. Staring down the inlet, though he could now see nothing of the *Alice*, he voiced his anger at the men who had left him.

"They put back for two *Tommies* and then leave me like I didn't even belong to the ship. Wait till I see 'em again. Just wait, the . . . argh!" he spat out in disgust.

Taking off his jumper he wrung as much water from it as possible, then donned it again. From the overturned tank there were no signs of life. The men inside must have been badly injured when it overturned; they were either dead or unconscious. Slugger felt as if he were the only one alive.

For half an hour he sat there disconsolate, not knowing what to do. Then he heard voices, and from the south end of the jetty, less than forty yards away, several German soldiers appeared. They dodged from shelter to shelter, and each carried a sub-machine gun.

Slugger huddled closer to the beach and realised for the first time that if he were seen he would become a prisoner-of-war. It gave him a distinct shock. Until then he had only been angry at his comrades for forsaking him. Now cold fear took the place of anger. P.O.W. The three letters had a frightening ring about them.

He watched the soldiers scurry from point to point, keeping under cover as much as possible in case the raiders had left a party behind. Finally convinced that they had really gone, the Germans came out into the open and stood staring at the tank.

Then for the next twenty minutes they worked to free the trapped men. Slugger watched as they pulled out the limp bodies, one after another.

A few minutes later an officer appeared and began to organise the soldiers into a fire-fighting team. Buckets were brought from the houses untouched by the fire and a bucket-line formed. It was then that Slugger saw something which gave him hope. To get to the water one of the soldiers dropped into a boat moored at the quay. From it he could fill the buckets and hand them up to a comrade above him and so to the bucket gang. Slugger watched and planned. That boat could take him to safety.

The work of fire-fighting went on for two hours, and Slugger became progressively colder as his clothes dried on him. Steadily the glow from the house fires dimmed.

Finally the officer must have been satisfied that there was no chance of the fires springing to life again, for the soldiers collected the arms they had put down, and marched away. Slugger, shivering, shook himself. If he could get a boat, and if it was a motor boat, then his chances were good. After a night like this the Germans were not likely to return to the waterfront.

He waited until everything was quiet and the only sounds were those made by the tiny waves lapping against the slime-covered piles on which the quay had been built. Moving slowly and testing the gravel with each foot, he began to make his way across to the quay.

He had gone only a few paces along the quay when he stepped on a loose board. It sprang under his weight and from the darkness masking the centre of the quay came a sharp query and the ominous click as a gun was cocked. The Germans had left a sentry! Slugger stood his ground, hoping that if the German heard nothing more he might believe he had imagined the sound. His heart thumping, Slugger waited, straining his ears to catch the least sound. After a moment or

His heart thumping, Slugger waited . . .

so he heard voices as if two men were discussing the sound they had heard. Expecting any moment to have a torch flicked on and the light shone on him, Slugger waited. He had no weapons, so he could not attack first.

He waited and waited, and nothing happened. The two German sentries were nervous. When they drove down to this lonely fishing village that afternoon it had seemed to them as if the war in Greece was over. They had evacuated the villagers and begun to make themselves comfortable. Then, with dusk, had come this sudden attack from the sea.

The overturned tank was evidence enough that the British were not beaten. They had come here for some unknown reason, blasted the quay and gone away. Whether they had left men behind to commit sabotage neither sentry knew, and both were afraid that if they made a move a burst of bren gun fire from the darkness might mow them down.

" We should go behind the houses, Erich," one of them said, " and so take them in the rear."

Erich grunted.

"I think we should move back to the houses and stay there," he suggested. "If they come out on to the quay, we are then sheltered and can shoot without being shot. These British are devils at close fighting."

They moved silently away from the quay edge to the shadows of the nearby buildings and waited, fingers tense on triggers. At the other end of the quay Slugger also waited, and waited. Finally, lowering himself to his hands and knees, and feeling cautiously ahead of him for loose boards, he crawled away from the sea's edge towards the even thicker shadows of the nearest house.

It took quarter of an hour, and the goose-pimples were chasing up his cheeks all the time. He kept expecting the silence to be shattered by a fusillade of shots. When he finally reached the shelter of the nearest building he was sweating again.

He was playing a game of Blind Man's Buff, with the risk of a bullet if he made a false move or a sound. He had to get to the opposite end of the quay. Then there would be the risk of making a sound as he got into the boat. It seemed hopeless, yet he kept on. He moved along the back of the building, stopped and listened, then crossed the open space to the next building. At last he was so close to the two houses which had been on fire that he could smell the wet charred woodwork.

Slowly he went round the end of the building. Now he was facing the water. The sides of the fjord showed blacker than the sky and the sea. Forty feet of quay lay between him and the water. Forty feet—and two German sentries on the quay itself.

"If only there was somebody else with me," he thought. "We could handle two men. I'll bet they're as scared as I am."

He was about to make his attempt when he heard the soft pad-pad-pad of feet. Only a man whose nerves were strung almost to breaking point could have picked up those sounds. Slugger shrank back into the darkness of the house wall, praying he would not be seen.

He counted shadows—five in all. Five men who went across the quay without making a single plank creak. That made Slugger feel worse. They passed as if they were ghosts.

Then there was a sound—a faint chink of wood on wood. The men were getting into the boat which Slugger had been planning to use. His hopes of escape died immediately. Probably they were a German patrol getting ready for a dawn patrol of the nearby beaches to stop further attempts at rescuing British stragglers.

Then came another sound. This time of men running—and they were making no attempt to move soundlessly. Slugger risked a peep round the corner on to the quay but shrank back again at once. The two sentries were rushing nearer, one swinging a torch and the other keeping behind him so that neither was shown up by their own light.

The Germans stopped about ten yards from the spot where the boat was moored. While one shone his torch down into the water so that it lit up the edge of the quay, the other snapped out a command and fired a shot just above the level of the quay. It was obviously a threat of what would follow if the men who had climbed down into the boat tried to resist.

There was a murmur of voices, then the Germans marched boldly forward. One threatened the men in the boat with his sub-machine gun, the other kept the torch trained on them.

Slugger ground his teeth. The shadowy figures had not been Germans setting out on a dawn patrol. They were either soldiers making a desperate attempt to get away or perhaps maybe Greek fishermen. He crouched in his hiding-place and watched the two Germans menace the unseen escapers.

The first of the men began to climb out on to the quay. Then Slugger Burton moved. It was a last, desperate attempt and he put every ounce of speed and strength into it.

Like a thunderbolt he tore across the quay. The two sentries must have heard him, for both started to turn. But they were not quick enough. Slugger thumped the man with the sub-machine gun in the solar plexus with his left and dealt the other a crisp right to the jaw.

Both went over and into the boat. There were yells of pain and fierce cries of anger. Slugger grabbed the torch which had fallen on to the quay and shone it into the boat. Five pairs of startled eyes stared up at him. The two sentries were not looking at anyone just then. One was down for the count thanks to Slugger's well-known crisp right. The other was writhing from the effects of the solar plexus punch.

" British . . . British," Slugger said, pointing to himself. " Anybody speak the lingo?"

The petrified Greek fishermen, all from the village, merely stared at him. Slugger grabbed the sub-machine gun lying at his feet and dropped nimbly into the boat. Threatening the Greeks with the gun, he forced them into the bows of the twenty-foot craft. He had already seen that there was a motor, and when the two Germans had been hauled into the bows, Slugger pointed his sub-machine gun at one of the Greeks, then pointed to the motor.

"Start it . . . we're going to Crete!"

It was the word Crete which unfroze the five men. They exchanged startled glances, muttered among themselves for a moment or so, then one made his way cautiously to the stern. He primed the engine, swung the handle and at the first turn, the engine came to life.

It was anything but a Rolls-Royce, and the thump-clunk-thumity-clunk as it started to warm up turned Slugger's blood cold. It seemed that the noise must be heard by every German soldier within miles. Yet when the screw had been put in gear and the mooring line cast off, they eased out into the darkness without interference from the shore.

When dawn came in they were almost twenty miles out to sea. The Germans had been trussed securely, and though none of the Greeks understood a word Slugger said to them, they were smiling as happily as he was. There was no doubt where they were going—to Crete, away from German-occupied Greece. It was evening before the rickety engine was switched off and the boat ground against the jetty at the port of Canea in Crete.

The soldier guarding that particular spot took them in for interrogation. The Greeks were still being questioned when Slugger was allowed to go and told where he could get a meal and a bed for the night.

There was no need to accept anybody's hospitality, however, for as he went out into the reddening light of the setting sun, ambulances were hurrying over to the quay where a badly battered anti-submarine ship had docked. It was the *Alice*!

Slugger watched the wounded men being brought ashore.

The last to be carried off the ship was the skipper, Lieutenant Otis Chambers. Slugger halted the stretcher bearers for a moment. Giving Otis Chambers a salute and hiding a grin, he said:

"Able Seaman Burton reporting back for duty, sir."

Otis Chambers was in pain. He had paid dearly for his trip to the wheel-house when the *Alice* was being pounded by the tank gun, and for him there would be no more

action at sea for a long time. He opened hi
eyes, stared at Slugger, then the taut pai
lines smoothed out.

"Well I'm dashed," he whispered. "Abl
Seaman Burton. We left you behind—by
mistake."

"Yessir," Slugger agreed, grinning. "I'n
sorry for being away without official leave."

"If I were fit I'd dock you a day's pay,"
Chambers said, and despite his pain he man
aged a grin. "As it is, all I can say is—
don't do it again. You might not be so lucky
next time. Goodbye—Slugger." And he
winked as the stretcher bearers carried him
away to the nearby ambulance.